Little Sally On Safari

Written and illustrated by T. Steele Petry

Printed in the United States of America
Library of Congress Control Number: 2020923239
ISBN: Softcover   978-1-64908-571-9
        eBook   978-1-64908-570-2
        Hardback   978-1-64908-572-6
Republished by: PageTurner Press and Media LLC
Publication Date: 12/10/2020

To order copies of this book, contact:

PageTurner Press and Media
Phone: 1-888-447-9651
order@pageturner.us
www.pageturner.us

Book review by Olivia Farr

"Little Sally loved her home where she could walk and talk with the animals."

Young readers can join little Sally as she travels around her home in Africa to visit the animals that live there. Unfortunately, along the way, little Sally gets lost, but she knows just who to ask to help her find her way back home. Luckily, Mrs. Giraffe is able to use her high vantage point to locate little Sally's home and point her in the right direction. The book tracks her journey as little Sally says hello to a lion, elephant, tiger, and several other animals.

Each two-page spread features text in a large font on one page with a large painting of the animal being discussed on the other page. There are plenty of colors to keep the attention of young children, and the text is not too lengthy for little ones, who will also enjoy the rhymes that appear throughout. For children who like animals and exploring, this is a fun picture book. The side plot of Sally getting lost and needing to find her way back home is also engaging. The book can spark discussions about what children should do if they should find themselves in a similar situation. This is an important topic for children, as knowing what do in these situations can be empowering.

Little Sally's fun journey to visit the animals in Africa is sure to spark the imaginations of the author's young readers. With colorful paintings of many animals and a cute story that is easy to read aloud, this is a delightful read for older toddlers and young elementary school children. Additionally, this can be an important discussion starter that can allow parents to teach children about what to do when they are lost.

Little Sally woke up in her far away home in a land called Africa.

Little Sally loved her home where she could walk and talk with the animals.

This morning Little Sally decided to go for a walk to visit her animal friends.

The first animal she met was Mr. Lion, resting in the grass.

"A very nice day", said Little Sally.

"Yes indeed, now please go and play" replied Mr. Lion.

And Little Sally walked away.

The second animals Little Sally found were two hippos playing happily in the river.

Little Sally decided not to bother the two, the father and his daughter.

And Little Sally walked away.

Little Sally next met Mr. Water Buffalo. He was always funny as he had little birds on his back.

"Good day" said Little Sally.

"Good day, sorry I cannot stay" replied Mr.

Water Buffalo as he waved his ears to go.

And Little Sally walked away.

Soon Little Sally came across Mr. Elephant and he looked very frightened.

"What's up in your house?" asked Little Sally.

"I saw a mouse!" replied Mr. Elephant.

"Oh, no worry!" said Little Sally.

"Maybe not, but gotta hurry!" replied Mr. Elephant as he thundered away.

And Little Sally walked away.

Little Sally walked on and soon found Mrs.

Leopard resting in a tree.

"What's new up there?" asked Little Sally. "Rain is in the air." replied Mr. Leopard. "Well have a very nice day!" said Little Sally.

"Time for a nap, no time to play" replied Mrs. Leopard as she yawned and turned away.

And Little Sally walked on.

Little Sally had walked a long way and soon felt she was lost and scared.

She looked about and saw Mr. Rhino in the grasslands.

He was very nice and she began to walk toward him when Mrs. Giraffe came along.

Mrs. Giraffe was so much taller and could see for a long way.

Little Sally walked to Mrs. Giraffe.

Little Sally asked Mrs. Giraffe, "Please help me find my way home!"

Mrs. Giraffe looked about and said "I see it and it is a very short roam."

And Little Sally walked home, happy with her visits of the day.

CPSIA information can be obtained
at www.ICGtesting.com
Printed in the USA
LVHW070237010221
677982LV00022B/570